For:
Raedyn
Merry Christmas
2020
Love,
GG & G-Pa

For the Tiny Chef inside every one of us.

RAZORBILL

An imprint of Penguin Random House LLC, New York

First published in the United States of America by Razorbill, an imprint of Penguin Random House LLC, 2020

Copyright © 2020 by Tiny Chef Productions LLC
Tiny Chef™ and the Tiny Chef logo are trademarks of Tiny Chef Productions LLC.

Visit us online at penguinrandomhouse.com

Library of Congress Cataloging-in-Publication
data is available.

Manufactured in China.

ISBN 9780593115053

1 3 5 7 9 10 8 6 4 2

Produced at Ancient Order of the Wooden Skull Productions • Production design by Jason Kolowski • Storyboards, illustrations, and compositing by Lance LaSpina • Sculpts by Hiroe Goto • Additional painting by Robyn Yannoukos and Sean Ghobad • Additional lighting design by Eric Atkins • Blegaful Shew recipe adapted for humans by Chef Laura Louise Oats • All other textures and ornaments courtesy of Shutterstock • Special thanks: Matt Hutchinson, the Larsen Family, Nell Reid, Kyle Arneson, Jack Zegarski, and especially Miss Penny

Design by Maggie Edkins • Text set in BlackBeard

The Tiny Chef

and da mishing weshipee blook

RACHEL LARSEN, ADAM REID, and OZI AKTURK

RAZORBILL

This lovely old stump,
on this ordinary street,
is home to a creature
you really must meet!

He loves games and music and especially books.
He is the Tiny Chef, and he lives to cook.

This is his kitchen, but what happened here?
What a disaster! Oh my word, oh my dear!

And where is the Chef
in this torn-apart stump?
If you look closely, you'll
spot just his rump.

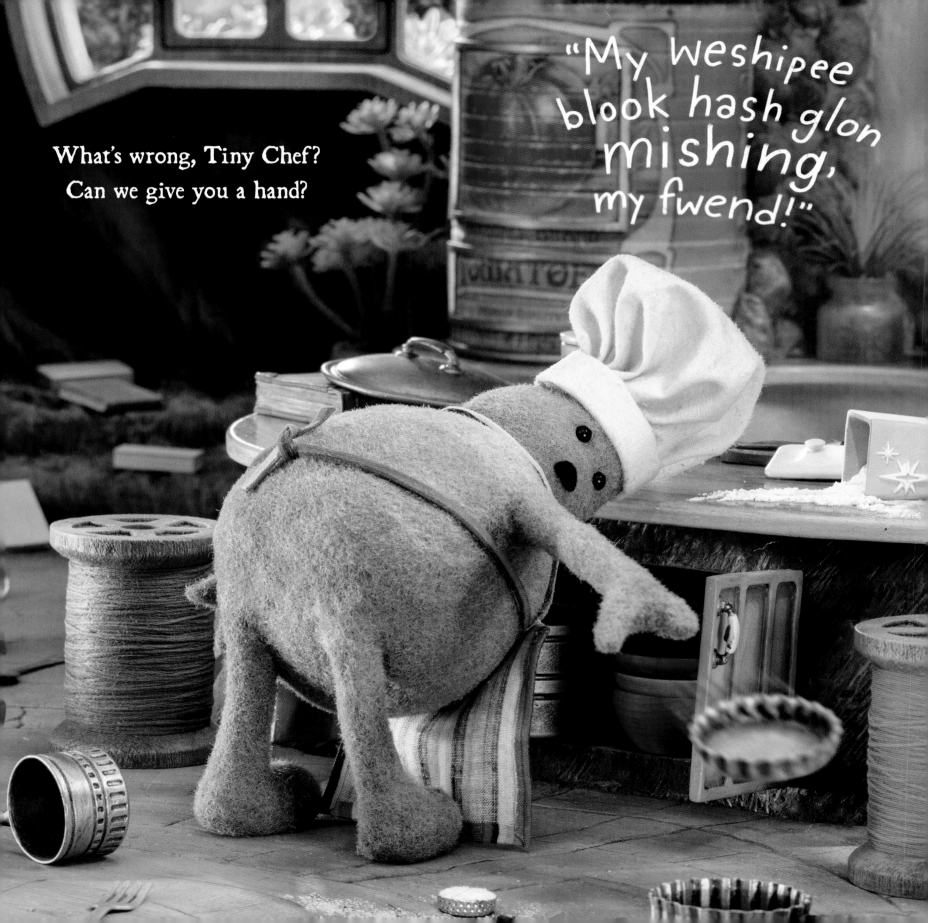

It finally happened.
Good golly, good gosh.
The Chef's precious recipe book
appears to be lost!

This book contains secrets to
Chef's VERY BEST dishes!
The creations he makes when he
feels most ambitious!

SEPTEMBER

MON	TUE	WED	THU	FRI	SAT
2 Cat cafay. Blall daylooooooong	**3**	**4** Bashel s's Mappy blirfday	**5** 5 days y mipinny's bl-day	**6** ♡	**7**
8	**9** ☺	**10** Mipinny blirfday!	**11**	**12** ☆	**13** Medifate	**14**
15 5 daysh blafter mipinny blirfday	**16** weewax	**17** Shkype Mish Jackie, wash golen girlsh	**18**	**19**	**20**	**21** Bloat cweaturesh
22	**23**	**24** pawluck pawty BWING PIESH	**25** SHkype Mish pinny	**26**	**27** peshto pashta wi mushwoooooomsh ooooovioushly	**28**
29	**30** gharlden					

Like the Blegaful Mie
he makes once a year
on the first day of fall,
and that day is here.

So he looks in his fridge and in other odd places,
like under his bed, and in dark, smelly spaces.

With no book in sight,
the Chef throws quite a tantrum:

"I fannot meleeve
dish mashally
haffumed!"

Count down from ten, Chef.
Let all worry go.
Let's take a deep breath
and let it out slow.

His herb garden forest is just steps away,
and towers above him with branches that sway.

The smell in the air
of rosemary and thyme
makes his clipping and snipping
well worth the climb.

On the mushroom trail with its damp, grassy floor.
Oh, what a harvest, portobellos galore!
How can he resist? He takes some to go.
So tasty and hearty, as our Tiny Chef knows.

Back at the stump,
the Chef dumps out his haul
and begins the big task
of making it small.

He slices some garlic as thin as he can.
Then sautés it up in his bottle-cap pan.
He mixes in mushrooms, potatoes, then stirs,
tossing in carrots, some celery, and herbs.

The Tiny Chef sings as he gleefully cooks.
He's forgotten all about his lost recipe book.
He straightens his hat—the stew now needs to simmer...

So he keeps himself busy singing songs about dinner.
Waiting is hard with a rumbling tummy,
but he knows that the waiting will make it more yummy.

When the moment arrives,
the Chef gives it a try.
It's...SO DELICIOUS
he actually cries.

And that's when his recipe book finally appears!

Right where he'd left it!
Now, isn't that weird?

The Chef can't believe it!
His little heart bursts.
It was there all along—
did you see it first?

Now the Tiny Chef knows just what to do
with his new favorite recipe, Blegaful Shew.
He wrote all the steps down as best as he could,
then found a blank page and taped it in good.

The Chef realized he'd learned so much today
about feeling lost and then finding his way.
Staying inspired is truly an art,
and the very best recipes . . .
come straight from the heart.